This book is dedicated in loving memory, to my brother, Michael John Luedke, (1952-2005). More than any other person I've known, Mike's life embodied the qualities demonstrated by our Lord. Compassionate, persistent, loving and most of all, a servant to those in need. His selflessness was contagious to any who came to know him. He was a man to be admired, because he had never sought to be!

EYE WITNESS (BOOK TWO):
Acts of the Spirit

By
Robert James Luedke

21st CENTURY COLORS:
CARSTEN BRADLEY

1st CENTURY COLORS:
ROBERT LUEDKE

COVER RENDERING: TOMMY CASTILLO
COVER PAINTING: CARSTEN BRADLEY
COVER DESIGN: ROBERT LUEDKE

PRODUCTION ASSISTANCE:
MICHAEL ANTHONY LAGOCKI
JAY PETERANETZ

Eye Witness: Acts of the Spirit, Copyright 2006, Robert James Luedke.
Published by Head Press Publishing: 2201 Long Prairie Road, Suite 107-770, Flower Mound, TX 75022.

FIRST EDITION ISBN: 0-9758924-2-8

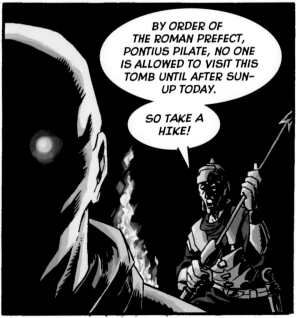

1

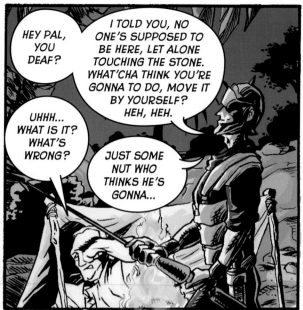

2

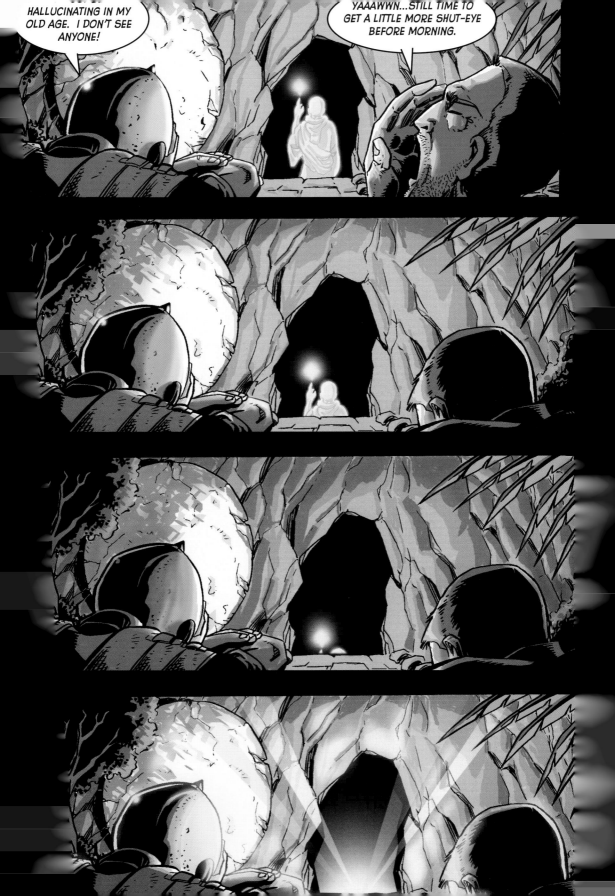

JOURNAL ENTRY DR. TERRANCE HARPER...7/24/04   7:05 PM

-RE : NOTES ON OUTCOME OF JERUSALEM TRIP AT REQUEST OF DR. RIBAN

   -MY ASSISTANT, RAJ PATEL, AND I HAVE BEEN A PARTY TO ONE OF THE GREATEST DISCOVERIES IN MODERN ARCHAEOLOGY! WORKING WITH THE ISRAELI MINISTRY OF ANTIQUITIES, WE HAVE PROVIDED VALUABLE INFORMATION THAT LED TO THE TRANSLATION OF A FIRST CENTURY PAPYRUS, WHICH WAS FOUND WITHIN AN OSSUARY DISCOVERED BY SEISMIC RESEARCHERS BENEATH THE FOUNDATIONS OF MODERN DAY JERUSALEM. AT THIS JUNCTURE, THE PAPYRUS APPEARS TO BE A PREVIOUSLY UNKNOWN MANUSCRIPT DETAILING THE LAST VISIT TO JERUSALEM OF THE MAN THE WORLD KNOWS AS JESUS OF NAZARETH. THROUGH THE NARRATIVE, MUCH OF THE INFORMATION CONTAINED WITHIN THE BIBLICAL ACCOUNTS APPEARS TO BE CONFIRMED, AND IT ALSO SHEDS ADDITIONAL LIGHT ON SOME OF THE SOCIO-POLITICAL ELEMENTS SURROUNDING THIS EVENT.

   -BASED ON THE FACT THAT THE DOCUMENT APPEARS TO BE IN THE ORIGINAL AUTHOR'S HAND, (AND CARBON DATED TO THE MID-FIRST CENTURY), IT IS AN UNPRECEDENTED FIND THAT WILL SERVE TO ANSWER THE ARGUMENT RAISED BY SKEPTICS OVER THE YEARS, THAT THE BIBLICAL ACCOUNTS HAD BEEN INFLUENCED BY LEGEND AND SENSATIONALISM OVER CENTURIES OF RE-TRANSLATIONS.

   *-AS AN ADDED BONUS, THE OSSUARY CONTAINED A TRIO OF CORRODED STEEL SPIKES, WHICH ARE REFERENCED IN THE NARRATIVE AS BEING THE ACTUAL NAILS USED IN JESUS' CRUCIFIXION! DO WE NOW HAVE A BLOOD-SAMPLE AND DNA FROM JESUS? ANALYSIS IS STILL PENDING ON THIS.

9:15pm: -AFTER A DINNER MEETING WITH DR. RIBAN, IT APPEARS THAT THE OFFICIAL POSITION OF THE ISRAELI GOVERNMENT IS, THIS DISCOVERY WILL NOT BE REVEALED TO THE PUBLIC AT THIS TIME...POSSIBLY NEVER...DESPITE THE CONSENSUS OPINION OF ITS AUTHENTICITY AMONG THOSE IN ATTENDANCE!

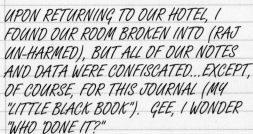

UPON RETURNING TO OUR HOTEL, I FOUND OUR ROOM BROKEN INTO (RAJ UN-HARMED), BUT ALL OF OUR NOTES AND DATA WERE CONFISCATED...EXCEPT, OF COURSE, FOR THIS JOURNAL (MY "LITTLE BLACK BOOK"). GEE, I WONDER "WHO 'DONE IT?'"

7/25/04 5:17AM

RE: EXIT STRATEGY-JERUSALEM

RAJ & I ARE READY TO LEAVE FOR THE AIRPORT. I HAVE MADE ARRANGEMENTS FOR THIS BOOK (ALONG WITH ITS HIDDEN WIRELESS VIDEO RECORDER, WHICH CONTAINS A RECORDING OF THE ENTIRE TRANSLATION SESSION OF 7/23/04), TO BE FEDX'D TO RAJ'S WIFE, CYNTHIA PATEL. IN THE EVENT THAT WE DO NOT MAKE IT SAFELY OUT OF ISRAEL, THIS WILL ENSURE THAT THIS INFORMATION WILL BE REVEALED TO MY COLLEAGUES AND THE WORLD. CYNTHIA IS DIRECTED TO FORWARD THIS BOOK TO MR. CURTIS McINTYRE IN NEW YORK...

OH MY GOD!

DEAR LORD, PLEASE PROTECT THEM BOTH AND BRING RAJ SAFELY HOME TO US!

DAD-DEE?

ONE DAY EARLIER...

HEY KID, HANDS OFF M'CAB!

I GO TO THE SWEET LIFE WHERE FLOWS A RIVER OF HONEY...

OH, NO!

5

THERE'S SO MUCH SMOKE AND DUST THAT MORNING LOOKS LIKE NIGHT.

THE ONLY SOUND I CAN HEAR IS A CONSTANT RINGING IN MY EARS.

AS THE SMOKE BEGINS TO DISSIPATE...

...THE REALIZATION OF WHAT HAS HAPPENED BEGINS TO SETTLE IN...

...AND I TRY TO SCREAM.

BUT NOTHING COMES OUT...

...AND THEN EVERYTHING WENT WHITE!

11

WELL, THAT'S WHERE I COME IN.

WHILE JOSEPH DID A WONDERFUL JOB OF JOURNALIZING THE LAST WEEK OF JESUS' MORTAL EXISTENCE, AS DID OUR BROTHERS MATTHEW, MARK AND JOHN...THAT'S ONLY THE BEGINNING OF THIS STORY, NOT THE ENDING!

I WAS UNIQUELY CHARGED BY GOD WITH THE RESPONSIBILITY OF RECORDING JESUS' RETURN AND THE ARRIVAL OF GOD'S COUNSELOR ON EARTH.

COUNSELOR? WHO'S THE COUNSELOR?

THE COUNSELOR IS THE **HOLY SPIRIT OF TRUTH** OF WHICH BOTH JESUS AND THE ANCIENT HEBREW SCRIPTURES HAD FORETOLD. I AM THE CHRONICLER OF THE ACTIONS OF THIS **HOLY SPIRIT**!

TO PUT IT IN MORE CONTEMPORARY TERMS, YOU MIGHT SAY I'M THE GHOST OF EASTERS PAST!

VERY FUNNY. A SPECTRE WITH A SENSE OF HUMOR...I LIKE THAT!

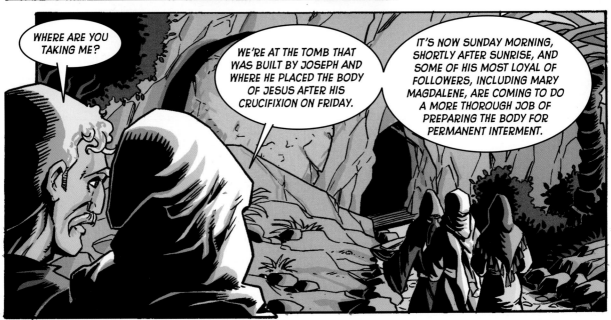

WHERE ARE YOU TAKING ME?

WE'RE AT THE TOMB THAT WAS BUILT BY JOSEPH AND WHERE HE PLACED THE BODY OF JESUS AFTER HIS CRUCIFIXION ON FRIDAY.

IT'S NOW SUNDAY MORNING, SHORTLY AFTER SUNRISE, AND SOME OF HIS MOST LOYAL OF FOLLOWERS, INCLUDING MARY MAGDALENE, ARE COMING TO DO A MORE THOROUGH JOB OF PREPARING THE BODY FOR PERMANENT INTERMENT.

14

15

17

BUT DUE TO THE INCREDIBLE NATURE OF THEIR REPORT AND THE FACT THAT THE TESTIMONY OF WOMEN COUNTED FOR VERY LITTLE AT THIS TIME IN OUR HISTORY, MOST DID NOT BELIEVE.

WHAT NONSENSE IS THIS THAT YOU SPEAK OF WOMAN?

IT MUST BE WINE. THEY'VE DRUNKEN TOO MUCH IN THEIR GRIEF.

THAT IS, ALL BUT ONE!

PETER, DO YOU PUT ANY STOCK IN THEIR STORY?

WELL..?

WITHOUT SAYING A WORD, PETER RUNS FROM THE HOUSE...

WHERE ARE YOU GOING? YOU KNOW IT'S TOO DANGEROUS FOR US OUT ON THE STREETS RIGHT NOW!

I'LL BE OKAY, JAMES!

... AND THROUGH THE STREETS OF JERUSALEM.

18

HE TRAVELS PAST THE POTTER'S FIELD JUST OUTSIDE THE CITY'S WALLS, WHERE THE TRAITOROUS APOSTLE, JUDAS ISCARIOT, IS STILL HANGING FROM THE TREE WHERE HE TOOK HIS OWN LIFE IN SHAME .

JUDAS HAD PURCHASED THIS PATCH OF LAND WITH PART OF THE "BLOOD MONEY" PAID TO HIM FOR HIS BETRAYAL OF JESUS.

ONCE THIS BECAME KNOWN BY THE PEOPLE, THE FIELD WAS FOREVERMORE REFERED TO AS, "AKELDAMA", OR THE FIELD OF BLOOD.

THE SCRIPTURES HAD TO BE FULFILLED!

"MAY THIS PLACE BE DESERTED. LET NO ONE DWELL IN IT."

HE RUNS LIKE A MAN POSSESSED NON-STOP ALMOST TWO KILOMETERS, UNTIL HE REACHES THE TOMB ENTRANCE.

THIS IS IMPOSSIBLE! THE LINEN BURIAL STRIPS LAY NEATLY IN PLACE, EXACTLY WHERE HIS BODY SHOULD BE.

IF HE WERE STRIPPED OF THEM, OR IF HE REMOVED THEM HIMSELF, ONE WOULD THINK THEY'D BE RANDOMLY TOSSED ABOUT THE TOMB?

YES, THAT WOULD SEEM TO MAKE PERFECT SENSE, PETER.

EH?

BUT WHAT IS IMPOSSIBLE WITH MAN...

20

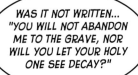

22

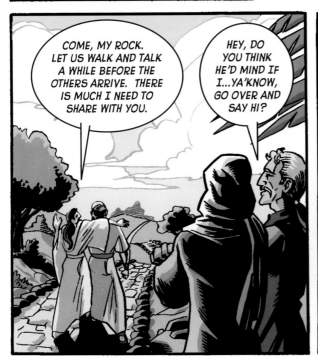

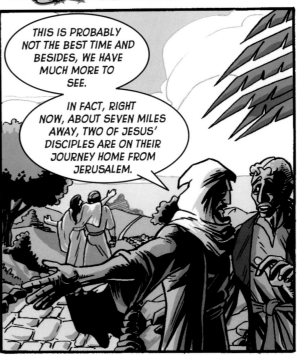

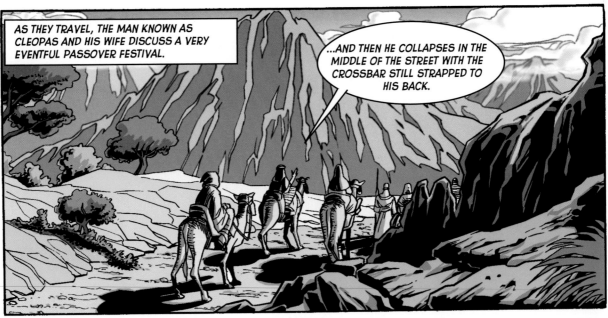

AS THEY TRAVEL, THE MAN KNOWN AS CLEOPAS AND HIS WIFE DISCUSS A VERY EVENTFUL PASSOVER FESTIVAL.

...AND THEN HE COLLAPSES IN THE MIDDLE OF THE STREET WITH THE CROSSBAR STILL STRAPPED TO HIS BACK.

WHAT DID THE ROMANS DO THEN?

CAN YA' BELIEVE IT? THEY GRABBED A GUY OUT OF THE CROWD...

...AND MADE HIM CARRY THE CROSSBAR ALL THE WAY TO GOLGOTHA.

GREETINGS TO YOU ON THIS FINE MORNING. WHAT IS IT THAT YOU ARE DISCUSSING?

THE AMAZING THINGS THAT HAPPENED IN JERUSALEM THESE LAST FEW DAYS, STRANGER.

THINGS? TO WHAT THINGS DO YOU REFER, FRIEND?

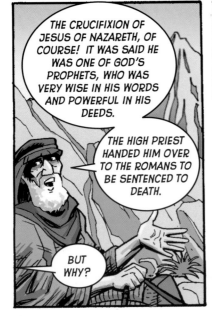

THE CRUCIFIXION OF JESUS OF NAZARETH, OF COURSE! IT WAS SAID HE WAS ONE OF GOD'S PROPHETS, WHO WAS VERY WISE IN HIS WORDS AND POWERFUL IN HIS DEEDS.

THE HIGH PRIEST HANDED HIM OVER TO THE ROMANS TO BE SENTENCED TO DEATH.

BUT WHY?

BECAUSE MANY OF US BELIEVED HE WAS THE MESSIAH, COME TO LEAD US OUT FROM THE BONDAGE OF ROME. WHAT'S MORE, HE HAD CLAIMED THAT DEATH COULD NOT OVERCOME HIM AND IF KILLED, HE WOULD RETURN FROM THE DEAD!

WOW!

THAT'S A PRETTY INCREDIBLE CLAIM TO MAKE!

24

26

THE NEXT DAY AFTER RETURNING TO JERUSALEM, THEY WENT TO SPEAK WITH **THE ELEVEN** AND SOME OF JESUS' OTHER DISCIPLES

...AND HE EVEN SAT AND BROKE BREAD WITH US!

THEN IT'S TRUE. JESUS HAS RISEN AND IS AMONG US!

BAH...HOW CAN WE ACCEPT THIS TESTIMONY WITHOUT ANY PROOF?

WHY DO YOU DOUBT THEM, BROTHER?

YOU ARE NOT FAMILIAR TO ME, SIR. WHO ARE YOU TO ADVISE US ON THESE ISSUES?

PEACE BE WITH ALL OF YOU, MY CHILDREN!

STAY BACK!

IT...IT'S A GHOST!

IT MAY BE SATAN TRYING TO TRICK US.

HE WAS PUT TO DEATH IN THE BODY, BUT MADE ALIVE IN THE SPIRIT.

27

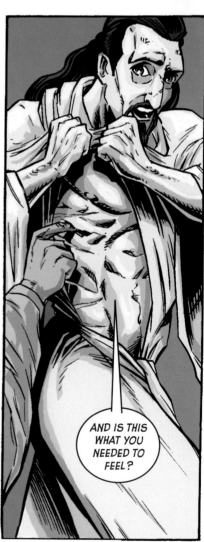

29

30

31

AS JESUS CONTINUES TO BLESS HIS FOLLOWERS, HE IS LIFTED UP BEFORE THEIR EYES BY A BRILLIANT LIGHT...UP INTO THE HEAVENS... AND VANISHES FROM THEIR SIGHT.

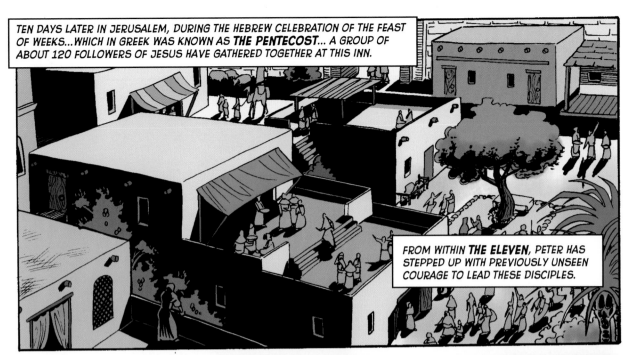

TEN DAYS LATER IN JERUSALEM, DURING THE HEBREW CELEBRATION OF THE FEAST OF WEEKS...WHICH IN GREEK WAS KNOWN AS **THE PENTECOST**... A GROUP OF ABOUT 120 FOLLOWERS OF JESUS HAVE GATHERED TOGETHER AT THIS INN.

FROM WITHIN **THE ELEVEN**, PETER HAS STEPPED UP WITH PREVIOUSLY UNSEEN COURAGE TO LEAD THESE DISCIPLES.

SUDDENLY, THE SKIES TURN DARK AND A VIOLENT WIND BLOWS THROUGHOUT THE CITY.

LOOKS LIKE WE'RE IN FOR A BIT OF A STORM. BETTER GET EVERYONE UNDER COVER, JAMES.

YEAH.

WOW, I DON'T REMEMBER EVER FEELING A WIND SO POWERFUL!

COME ON EVERYONE, LET'S GET INSIDE.

I'VE NEVER SEEN THE SKY BECOME SO DARK, SO QUICKLY?

WHAT'S HAPPENING, LUKE? THIS DOESN'T SEEM LIKE A NORMAL STORM.

YOU ARE ABOUT TO SEE A WONDROUS THING!

LOOK, UP IN THE SKY!

WITHOUT WARNING, WHAT APPEAR TO BE **TONGUES OF FIRE**, ARC DOWN FROM THE HEAVENS AND REST UPON EACH OF THE ELEVEN APOSTLES...

...PLUS ONE!

YEE...AHHHHH!

YEE...AHHHHH!

ALL RIGHT, IT LOOKS LIKE WE'VE GOT HIM BACK!

PULSE RATE IS 54 AND RISING STEADILY.

GOOD! GET HIM BACK ON THE I.V.S RACHEL, WE WANT TO MAKE SURE WE KEEP HIM STABILIZED.

WHA...WHAT IS IT?...WHAT HAPPENED?

YOU WERE HAVING A HEART ATTACK, BUT WE WERE ABLE TO GET YOU BACK ON-LINE WITH IMMEDIATE DEFIBRILLATION.

HOW LONG HAVE I...?

WE'VE KEPT YOU IN A MEDICALLY-INDUCED COMA FOR THE PAST TWO DAYS, IN THE HOPES IT WOULD HELP SPEED UP THE HEALING PROCESS.

YOUR VITAL SIGNS HAD APPEARED STRONGER, BUT OBVIOUSLY YOU'RE STILL NOT OUT OF THE WOODS YET.

BUT WHAT WAS THAT? IT FELT LIKE AN ELECTRIC CHARGE SHOOTING THROUGH ME.

THAT WAS THE DEFIB'...WE JUMP-STARTED YOUR HEART.

NO, NO... NOT THAT. WHAT WAS THAT BOLT OF ENERGY FROM THE CLOUDS?

TYPICAL HALLUCINATORY REACTION FROM THE MEDS.

YES, DOCTOR.

DR. LUCAS, THIS IS **AMON SEHED**, A COLLEAGUE AND FRIEND OF DR. HARPER, AND THIS IS **COMMANDER JUDITH ARYEH**, WITH THE TERRORISM DIVISION OF THE JERUSALEM POLICE FORCE.

IT'S A TERRIBLE SHAME ABOUT THE BOY! IS HARPER GOING TO PULL THROUGH?

IT'S STILL A BIT TOUCH AND GO AT THIS POINT, MINISTER RIBAN.

I THOUGHT WE WERE MAKING SIGNIFICANT PROGRESS, THAT IS, UP UNTIL THIS HEART ATTACK...VERY UNEXPECTED!

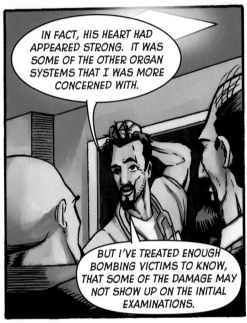

IN FACT, HIS HEART HAD APPEARED STRONG. IT WAS SOME OF THE OTHER ORGAN SYSTEMS THAT I WAS MORE CONCERNED WITH.

BUT I'VE TREATED ENOUGH BOMBING VICTIMS TO KNOW, THAT SOME OF THE DAMAGE MAY NOT SHOW UP ON THE INITIAL EXAMINATIONS.

I CANNOT BELIEVE THIS HAPPENED TO TERRY. SOMEONE MUST BE MADE TO PAY FOR THIS TRAGEDY!

AND THEY WILL, AMON, THAT I PROMISE YOU.

WHEN WILL HE BE ABLE TO GIVE ME A STATEMENT, DOCTOR?

IT MAY BE SEVERAL DAYS YET, COMMANDER.

HE'S STILL VERY WEAK, AND PRETTY OUT OF IT, BECAUSE OF THE MEDS.

ARE YOU TREATING THIS AS ANOTHER RANDOM ACT OF TERRORISM AGAINST ISRAEL?

THAT'S HOW IT APPEARS, BUT STRANGELY ENOUGH NO GROUP HAS COME FORWARD TO CLAIM RESPONSIBILITY YET.

IT MAY BE NOTHING, BUT HARPER KEEPS REFERRING TO A MISSION. IT COULD JUST BE PART OF A HALLUCINATION, BUT I WONDERED...

WHY DO YOU ASK?

WAIT JUST A MINUTE! DR. HARPER WAS HERE AT MY REQUEST TO AID THE MINISTRY OF ANTIQUITIES IN RESEARCH, NOTHING MORE. HE'S KNOWN INTERNATIONALLY FOR HIS WORK IN FORENSIC ARCHEOLOGY...

...HE'S NOT **JAMES BOND**, FOR GOODNESS SAKES!

ALL THE SAME, WE'LL NEED TO PURSUE EVERY POSSIBLE LEAD ON THIS CASE UNTIL WE CAN ESTABLISH A CLEAR MOTIVE FOR THE ATTACK...SIMPLE TERRORISM OR OTHERWISE.

DR. LUCAS, WILL YOU HAVE TIME TO GIVE ME A BRIEF STATEMENT ON THIS?

SURE. CAN WE MEET UP IN THE PHYSICIAN'S LOUNGE? I WANT TO STAY CLOSE TO THE HOSPITAL.

IT MIGHT BE HELPFUL TO THE INVESTIGATION, IF I UNDERSTOOD THE EXACT NATURE OF DR. HARPER'S VISIT.

VERY GOOD. I'LL MEET YOU THERE IN TWO HOURS. AND DR. RIBAN...I'D LIKE TO GET A STATEMENT FROM YOU, ALSO!

A STATEMENT FROM ME?

OH, UM...YES, YES OF COURSE!

ANYTHING TO HELP OUT.

YOU CAN COUNT ON OUR FULL COOPERATION.

WILL YOU TELL HER ABOUT THE SCROLLS...ABOUT WHAT HARPER REVEALED?

OF COURSE NOT. THAT INFORMATION IS NOT GERMANE TO THIS SITUATION.

39

NO ONE KNOWS ABOUT THIS DISCOVERY OUTSIDE OF OUR TEAM AND HARPER DID NOT PLACE ANY CALLS

BUT HOW CAN YOU BE SO SURE?

WE HAD THE PHONES TAPPED AT HIS HOTEL.

YOU WHAT?

JOSHUA, HOW COULD YOU DO SUCH A THING? TERRY HARPER IS A MAN OF UNQUESTIONABLE INTEGRITY!

I JUST CAN'T BELIEVE...

WHERE SOMETHING OF THIS LEVEL OF IMPORTANCE IS CONCERNED, I WILL GO TO ANY LENGTHS TO PROTECT THE PEOPLE OF ISRAEL...

...FROM ALL POTENTIAL ENEMIES!

DR. LUC, COULD I GET A MOMENT OF YOUR TIME?

SURE, MIA...WHAT DO YOU NEED?

IT'S RACHEL, I'M AFRAID THERE'S SOMETHING WRONG WITH HER.

YEAH, I NOTICED THE SAME THING. SHE SAYS IT'S JUST OVER-WORK...BUT YOU KNOW HER.

OUTSIDE OF HER SON, NURSING IS HER MAIN PASSION IN LIFE.

BUT THAT'S JUST IT...I THINK SOMETHING'S GOING ON WITH HER SON!

NATHAN? WHAT DO YOU SUSPECT?

ONE HOUR LATER...

YOUR COLLEAGUES, DRS. RIBAN AND SEHED, WERE HERE TO VISIT YOU EARLIER, ALONG WITH THE POLICE.

I TOLD THEM YOU'RE FAR TOO WEAK TO SPEAK WITH ANYONE YET.

UHHHH...

RIBA...RIBAAAA... OH, SO TIRED CAN'T EVEN THINK STRAIGHT.

THAT'S OKAY, TERRY. JUST GIVE INTO IT.

SLEEP IS THE BEST THING FOR YOU RIGHT NOW.

I'LL BE RIGHT HERE BY YOUR SIDE, LOOKING AFTER YOU.

THAT'S GOOD TO KNOOOO....

HUH?

WHAT'S THAT BURNING SMELL? SOMEONE COOKIN' UP STEAKS?

OH YEAH, I REMEMBER NOW. THERE WAS THIS LIGHTNING STRIKE!

NOT EXACTLY! WHAT YOU'VE JUST SEEN IS THE PASSING OF THE HOLY SPIRIT TO THE APOSTLES.

THE HOLY SPIRIT?

YOU MENTIONED THAT BEFORE. WHAT MAKES A SPIRIT HOLY?

41

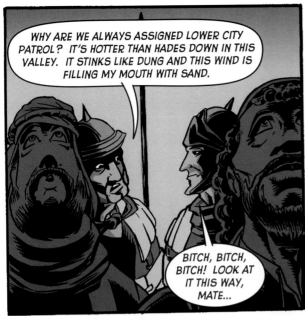

IN THE BLINK OF AN EYE, THE HEAVENS THEMSELVES SEEM TO OPEN UP, AS IF TO ANNOUNCE THE CLEANSING OF A WORLD THAT IS PREPARING FOR A NEW BEGINNING.

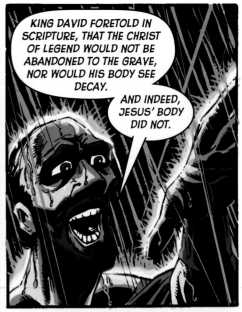

KING DAVID FORETOLD IN SCRIPTURE, THAT THE CHRIST OF LEGEND WOULD NOT BE ABANDONED TO THE GRAVE, NOR WOULD HIS BODY SEE DECAY.

AND INDEED, JESUS' BODY DID NOT.

JESUS OF NAZARETH WAS INDEED A MAN. HE WAS A CARPENTER BY TRADE, BUT A MAN WHO WAS ALSO ENDORSED BY GOD TO YOU, THROUGH THE MANY MIRACLES, HEALINGS AND SIGNS WHICH GOD PERFORMED AMONG YOU THROUGH HIM.

THIS MAN TOLD US WEEKS AGO THAT HE WOULD BE HANDED OVER TO YOU FOR GOD'S PURPOSE AND WITH HIS FOREKNOWLEDGE. HE FORETOLD THAT WITH THE HELP OF WICKED MEN, YOU WOULD HAVE HIM PUT TO DEATH BY NAILING HIM ON A CROSS.

BUT THIS MAN ALSO TOLD US THAT GOD WOULD RAISE HIM FROM THE GRAVE BECAUSE IT WAS IMPOSSIBLE FOR DEATH TO KEEP ITS HOLD ON HIM. MANY OF US HERE TODAY KNOW THIS TO BE A FACT, NOT BECAUSE WE'VE HEARD IT SAID, BUT BECAUSE WE ACTUALLY SAW HIM, TOUCHED HIM AND SPOKE WITH HIM.

GOD HAS RAISED JESUS IN BODY, MIND AND SPIRIT TO LIFE AFTER DEATH...

...AND THEN RECEIVED HIS RESURRECTED FORM AT HIS RIGHT HAND IN HEAVEN.

JESUS RECEIVED FROM THE FATHER **THE PROMISED HOLY SPIRIT** AND HAS NOW PASSED ITS MAGNIFICENCE ON TO HIS FOLLOWERS

THIS EVENT IS WHAT YOU HAVE JUST HEARD AND THIS IS WHAT YOU HAVE JUST WITNESSED.

44

THESE NEW DISCIPLES IMMEDIATELY DEVOTE THEMSELVES TO THE TEACHINGS OF JESUS AND FOLLOWING THE LIFESTYLE DEMONSTRATED BY THE APOSTLES.

I'M KIND OF FUZZY ON THE WHOLE MIRACLE CONCEPT. HOW DO YOU DEFINE A MIRACLE?

PEOPLE WITHIN JERUSALEM ARE AMAZED BY THE HEALINGS AND MIRACLES BEING PERFORMED ALMOST DAILY BY THE APOSTLES IN JESUS' NAME.

REMEMBER, THESE ARE THE SAME MEN, WHO JUST A FEW WEEKS BACK, WERE IN HIDING AND AFRAID TO EVEN SPEAK THE NAME OF JESUS IN PUBLIC, FOR FEAR OF BEING CONNECTED TO HIM.

YOU ARE ABOUT TO SEE FIRST HAND.

AS PETER AND JOHN ARE ENTERING THE OUTER COURTS OF THE TEMPLE, THEY ARE ABOUT TO HAVE AN ENCOUNTER WITH A MAN WHO IS WELL KNOWN IN THE CITY AND A FIXTURE AT THIS ENTRANCE LITERALLY FOR DECADES.

EVERY DAY HE IS CARRIED TO THIS GATE, CALLED BEAUTIFUL, TO BEG FROM THOSE ENTERING AND LEAVING THE TEMPLE COURTS.

SPARE A HALF A DENARIUS FOR A CRIPPLE, M'LORD?

NO!

NO?

LOOK AT ME!

I AM SIR.

47

48

49

CEASE THIS BLASPHEMY, GALILEAN...YOU ARE UNDER ARREST!

IT'S THE PHARISEE ENFORCER, SAUL OF TARSUS!

ON WHOSE AUTHORITY?

IN THE NAME OF CAIAPHAS, THE HIGH PRIEST, YOU ARE ACCUSED OF SPREADING THE PROHIBITED TEACHINGS OF THIS MAN, JESUS OF NAZARETH.

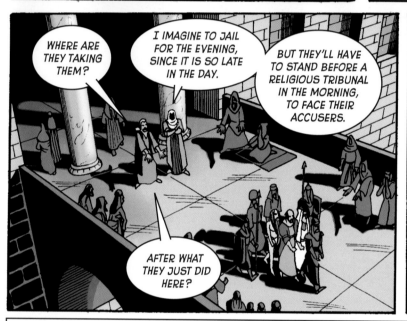

WHERE ARE THEY TAKING THEM?

I IMAGINE TO JAIL FOR THE EVENING, SINCE IT IS SO LATE IN THE DAY.

BUT THEY'LL HAVE TO STAND BEFORE A RELIGIOUS TRIBUNAL IN THE MORNING, TO FACE THEIR ACCUSERS.

AFTER WHAT THEY JUST DID HERE?

HOW COULD ANYONE NOT BELIEVE AFTER SEEING SOMETHING LIKE THAT?

MANY DO AND ARE ALREADY SPREADING WORD OF THIS EVENT AROUND THE CITY.

IN FACT, BY TOMORROW ANOTHER 2,000 PEOPLE WILL BECOME BELIEVERS.

THE NEXT MORNING, PETER AND JOHN ARE BROUGHT BEFORE THE SANHEDRIN, WHICH IS THE GOVERNING BODY THAT RULES OVER ALL HEBREW AFFAIRS IN JERUSALEM AND IS MADE UP OF PRIESTS, ELDERS AND RESPECTED TEACHERS OF THE LAW.

UNLIKE THE TRIALS OF JESUS, THIS WOULD BE A VERY WELL ATTENDED EVENT, DUE TO THE PUBLIC NATURE OF THE MIRACLES AND HEALINGS THE APOSTLES WERE PERFORMING ALL AROUND THE CITY.

51

HOW IS IT THIS UNSCHOOLED BRUTE SPEAKS SO ELOQUENTLY ABOUT THESE MATTERS?

HE'S A GALILEAN... A FISHERMAN FOR GOODNESS SAKES!

BUT ANNAS, HE HAS SPENT MANY YEARS UNDER HIS RABBI, THIS JESUS!

BUT WHAT HE IS SAYING IS SACRILEGE! ARE WE GOING TO STAND FOR THIS?

EVERYBODY IN THE CITY SEEMS AWARE OF THE OUTSTANDING MIRACLE THEY PERFORMED YESTERDAY AND WITH THE CRIPPLE STANDING HERE BEFORE US, WE CERTAINLY CANNOT DISPUTE IT.

THIS MOVEMENT MUST BE STOPPED BEFORE IT CAN SPREAD ANY FURTHER. THE FOLLOWERS OF THIS JESUS HAVE GATHERED THOUSANDS INTO THEIR RANKS IN JUST THE LAST FEW DAYS.

THEY SEEM TO BE GROWING STRONGER AFTER HIS DEATH, NOT WEAKER, LIKE WE HAD ASSUMED.

SAUL IS RIGHT! THEY ARE DEFYING THE UNOFFICIAL EDICT OF THIS COUNCIL, THAT BARS THE SPREADING OF THIS MAN'S TEACHINGS AND LIES OF HIS RESURRECTION. WE NEED TO MAKE A STRONG STATEMENT HERE!

LET'S STONE 'EM!

DON'T YOU SEE THIS CROWD?

ARE YOU NOT LISTENING TO THEM PRAISING GOD OVER THESE MEN ALL AROUND THE CITY?

TO CONDEMN THEM NOW, AFTER THE THINGS THEY'VE DONE, COULD SPARK A RIOT!

I AGREE, BUT YOU ARE THE SPIRITUAL LEADER OF ISRAEL, CAIAPHAS, NOT SOME FISHERMAN FROM GALILEE!

HMM...YES, YOU ARE RIGHT.

SO YOU MUST DEMONSTRATE THAT, BY MAKING AN OFFICIAL DECREE, THAT TO TEACH OR HEAL IN THIS MAN'S NAME IS TO COMMIT BLASPHEMY BEFORE GOD.

VERY WELL...THE COUNCIL HAS DECIDED THIS DAY TO BE MERCIFUL.

WE WILL SPARE YOU ANY PUNISHMENT FROM THIS MATTER, BUT LET ALL ISRAEL BE ADVISED...

...FROM THIS DAY FORWARD, TO SPEAK, HEAL OR TEACH IN THE NAME OF JESUS OF NAZARETH WITHIN THE WALLS OF JERUSALEM, IS OFFICIALLY CONSIDERED **BLASPHEMY**.

IT WILL BE VIEWED AS A DIRECT VIOLATION OF MY AUTHORITY, AS THE HIGH PRIEST OF GOD'S HOLY TEMPLE AND BE PUNISHABLE BY FLOGGING, IMPRISONMENT OR STONING.

JUDGE FOR YOURSELF WHETHER IT IS RIGHT **IN GOD'S SIGHT** TO OBEY YOU, RATHER THAN OBEY GOD...

...FOR WE CANNOT HELP SPEAKING IN TRUTH ABOUT WHAT WE HAVE SEEN AND HEARD.

HRRUMPH!

BOO...

BOO...

HISSS...

HRRUMPH!

THE COUNCIL HAS RULED.

THIS HEARING IS OVER!

53

IF IT WERE UP TO ME, GALILEAN, YOU'D BE DODGING CHUNKS OF GRANITE RIGHT NOW!

WELL THEN, SON OF TARSUS...

YESSS?

...I GUESS WE ARE FORTUNATE IT'S NOT UP TO YOU THEN...AREN'T WE?

MAKE SPORT OF ME WHILE YOU CAN, REBELS. BUT THE LORD IS MY WITNESS...

...MY TIME WILL COME!

...A ROMAN CITIZEN BY BIRTH AND A WEAVER AND TENT MAKER BY TRADE. BUT IN THIS PART OF THE EMPIRE, HE IS BETTER KNOWN BY HIS HEBREW NAME, **SAUL OF TARSUS**.

DON'T LET HIS GRUFF, WARRIOR-LIKE APPEARANCE FOOL YOU THOUGH...HE IS HIGHLY EDUCATED IN THE GREEK, ROMAN AND THE HEBREW CULTURES AND IS SAID TO BE ONE OF THE BRIGHTEST STUDENTS OF THE LEGENDARY RABBI, GAMALIEL.

HE IS FLUENT IN LATIN, GREEK, KOINE, HEBREW AND WHO KNOWS HOW MANY OTHER LANGUAGES AND DIALECTS.

HE IS AN UNYIELDING ADVOCATE OF THE CONSERVATIVE TRADITIONS OF THE PHARISEES AND HAS GAINED A REPUTATION AS BEING AN ENFORCER OF STRICT ADHERANCE TO MOSAIC LAW.

IT DOESN'T TAKE LONG FOR CAIAPHAS AND THE OTHER PRIESTS TO BECOME INCENSED BY THE APOSTLES BLATANT DISREGARD FOR THEIR PROCLAMATION AND ALSO JEALOUS OF ALL THE ATTENTION BEING PAID TO THEM BY THE PEOPLE, BECAUSE OF THE MIRACLES THEY CONTINUE TO PERFORM.

SO THEY ORDER THEIR ARREST...

...LEAD THEM THROUGH THE STREETS IN CHAINS...

...AND HAVE THEM IMPRISONED IN THE CITY'S DUNGEONS.

...AND JESUS SAID, THEY WILL DELIVER YOU TO SYNAGOGUES AND PRISONS AND ALL ON ACCOUNT OF ME.

...AND NOT A HAIR ON YOUR HEAD WILL PERISH.

APOSTLES OF JESUS...BREAK TIME'S OVER!

WHO ARE YOU?

IT IS TIME YOU TOOK YOUR PLACE ONCE AGAIN IN THE TEMPLE COURTS.

IT IS TIME TO RESUME TELLING THE PEOPLE THE FULL MESSAGE OF THIS NEW LIFE AND NEW COVENANT WITH GOD.

ZZZZ....

CLACK

COME, LET US LEAVE THIS PLACE.

THE NEXT MORNING, AT THE CHAMBERS OF THE SANHEDRIN.

LORD CAIAPHAS, I BRING URGENT NEWS!

WE WENT TO THE DUNGEON TO COLLECT THE FOLLOWERS OF JESUS, BUT THEY WERE NOT THERE.

WHAT?

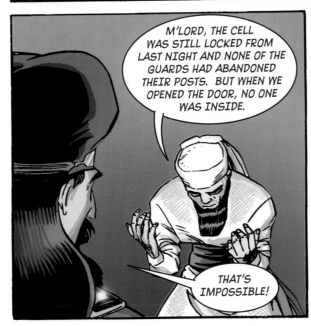

M'LORD, THE CELL WAS STILL LOCKED FROM LAST NIGHT AND NONE OF THE GUARDS HAD ABANDONED THEIR POSTS. BUT WHEN WE OPENED THE DOOR, NO ONE WAS INSIDE.

THAT'S IMPOSSIBLE!

HIGH PRIEST... THE MEN YOU PUT IN JAIL ARE BACK IN THE TEMPLE COURTS, INSTRUCTING IN THE FORBIDDEN TEACHINGS OF JESUS!

HOW CAN THIS BE?

59

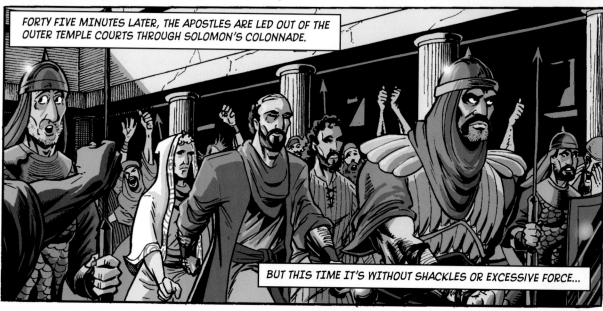

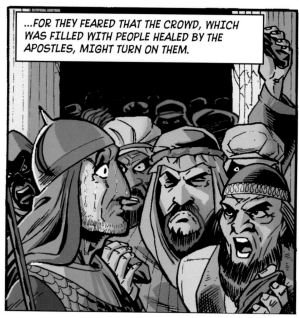

WE GAVE YOU STRICT ORDERS NOT TO TEACH IN THE NAME OF JESUS.

YET, YOU HAVE FILLED THE STREETS WITH YOUR LIES TO SUCH A DEGREE THAT PEOPLE ARE EVEN COMING HERE FROM OTHER CITIES TO LEARN MORE.

ARE YOU DETERMINED TO MAKE US GUILTY OF THIS MAN'S BLOOD, JAMES OF GALILEE?

NO... ...BUT ANNAS, WE MUST OBEY GOD, RATHER THAN LAWS MADE BY MAN.

YES, YOU HAD JESUS KILLED BY HANGING HIM ON A CROSS, BUT GOD RAISED HIM FROM THE DEAD...

...AND HE EXALTED HIM TO BE HIS RIGHT HAND, AS PRINCE AND SAVIOR...

...THAT HE MIGHT GIVE REPENTANCE AND FORGIVENESS OF SINS TO ALL OF ISRAEL THROUGH HIS NAME.

WE ARE ALL WITNESSES TO THESE THINGS AND SO IS THE HOLY SPIRIT, WHOM GOD HAS GIVEN TO THOSE WHO OBEY HIM!

AFTER MUCH DELIBERATION, WE HAVE DECIDED THAT THESE MEN MUST INDEED PAY A PRICE FOR DEFYING THE LAWS SET FORTH BY THIS COUNCIL.

BUT WE ALSO FEEL SOME MERCY IS WARRANTED. THEREFORE, THEY WILL NOT FACE A DEATH SENTENCE FOR THEIR BLASPHEMY, BUT RATHER, ACCORDING TO THE LAW, EACH WILL BE PUBLICLY FLOGGED.

YIPPEEE!

YA-HOOO

AMEN!

GOD HAS BLESSED YOU, BROTHERS!

DID I SAY THAT WRONG?

IT SOUNDED RIGHT TO ME.

HMMM?

OKAY, DID I MISS SOMETHING HERE? WHY ARE THEY CHEERING? THEY'RE GOING TO GET WHIPPED!

THESE MEN ARE THE FIRST TO SUFFER BECAUSE OF JESUS' NAME, AS HE SUFFERED FOR THEM ON THE CROSS!

THEY FEEL HONORED.

I'M NOT SURE I GET IT.

SELF-SACRIFICE IS INDEED A TOUGH CONCEPT TO DIGEST.

LET'S GET MOVIN'! THEY'RE WAITING ON YOU.

HUH? WHAT? HEY, WAIT A SEC!

JESUS HAD TOLD HIS APOSTLES THAT IF THEY WERE SUCCESSFUL AT SPREADING GOD'S NEW COVENANT, IT COULD LEAD TO PERSECUTION, TORTURE, IMPRISONMENT AND EVEN DEATH.

THEY SEE THIS SENTENCE AS EVIDENCE THAT THEY ARE BEING FAITHFUL TO GOD'S COMMAND FOR THEM.

AH, SIR? NO NEED FOR A HANDS-ON DEMONSTRATION. I'M ACTUALLY QUITE FAMILIAR WITH THE PROCEDURE!

MOVE IT, SCUM!

'SCUSE ME, BUT I REALLY DON'T BELONG HERE. I'M JUST AN OBSERVER.

LUKE, FEEL FREE TO CHIME IN AT ANY TIME.

LUKE, THIS ISN'T FUNNY!

LUKE!

AHHHH....

WHA-TSH

THAT'S ONE.

ARRRGGG!

WHA-TSH

TWO.

ARRRGGG!

THAT'S THE SECOND ONE.

65

WHA, WHAT IS IT...WHY ARE YOU WHIPPING ME?

WHIPPING YOU? HEH, HEH...NO, NOTHING QUITE THAT SERIOUS.

JUST CHECKING THE SUTURES ON YOUR RIB CONTUSIONS.

YOU'VE MADE SOME GOOD PROGRESS, TERRY. OUTSIDE OF A FLUCTUATING LIVER FUNCTION THAT I CAN'T SEEM TO PIN DOWN...

...WE MIGHT BE ABLE TO GET YOU OUT OF THE I.C.U. SOON.

I KNOW THE POLICE WANT TO TALK WITH YOU FIRST AND YOU MIGHT NOT FEEL UP TO THIS YET, BUT THERE'S SOMEONE HERE ANXIOUS TO SEE YOU.

I'LL ONLY ALLOW IT FOR A FEW MINUTES. YOU STILL NEED YOUR REST.

TERRY? HOW ARE YOU FEELING?

CYNTHIA?

CINDY, IS THAT YOU?

OH, TERRY, PRAISE GOD THAT YOU'RE STILL ALIVE! THE WAY THEY WERE TALKING, I THOUGHT I'D LOST YOU, ALSO.

I'M SO SORRY ABOUT RAJ. IT SHOULD HAVE BEEN ME!

DON'T SAY THAT TERRY.

I, I THOUGHT I GOT TO HIM IN TIME...TRIED TO THROW HIM CLEAR. I GUESS I WASN'T QUICK ENOUGH.

66

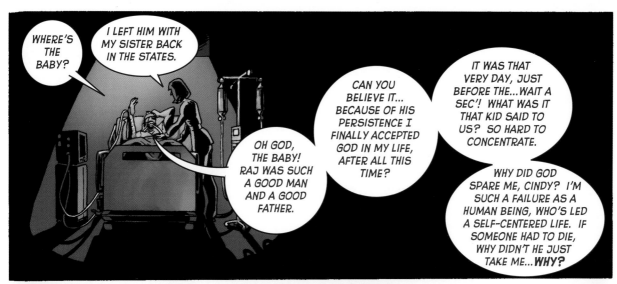

I CAN APPRECIATE YOUR BUSY SCHEDULE, DR. RIBAN, BUT IT'S IMPORTANT THAT I FULLY UNDERSTAND THIS SITUATION AND NEED YOUR INPUT, IT SEEMS, TO DO SO.

YES, OF COURSE... BUT CAN WE SPEED THIS ALONG? I DO HAVE A DINNER PLANNED WITH THE PRIME MINISTER THIS EVENING.

RIGHHHT!

THE AIRLINE'S RECORDS SHOW THAT DR. HARPER WAS BOOKED BY THE MINISTRY TO DEPART ISRAEL LESS THAN 40 HOURS AFTER ARRIVING.

WHY THE ABRUPT VISIT, MINISTER?

HE HAD SHARED HIS OPINION ON AN ARCHAEOLOGICAL DISCOVERY IN OUR POSSESSION AND WAS IN A HURRY TO RETURN TO HIS WORK IN THE STATES, I IMAGINE.

YOU KNOW THESE AMERICANS...ALWAYS IN A HURRY.

WHAT WAS THE EXACT NATURE OF THIS DISCOVERY THAT WARRANTED HIS INVOLVEMENT?

I'M AFRAID THAT INFORMATION IS CONSIDERED CLASSIFIED, MY DEAR...

...AND YOU DO NOT HAVE HIGH ENOUGH SECURITY CLEARANCE.

TERRIBLY SORRY!

DID DR. HARPER OR HIS COMPANION HAVE ANY ENEMIES IN ISRAEL THAT YOU ARE AWARE OF?

RIGHT.

A MAN OF HIS REPUTATION ALWAYS TENDS TO RUFFLE SOME PROFESSIONAL FEATHERS...

...BUT I DON'T KNOW OF ANY IRATE HUSBANDS LOOKING FOR HIM, IF THAT'S WHAT YOU MEAN... HEH, HEH!

68

NO, THAT'S NOT WHAT I MEAN, MINISTER.

TO PUT IT BLUNTLY...

...IS THERE ANYONE IN THE ARCHAEOLOGICAL COMMUNITY THAT MIGHT HAVE BENEFITTED FROM HARPER'S DEATH?

ARE YOU INFERRING THAT THIS MIGHT HAVE BEEN A TARGETED ATTACK?

THAT'S WHAT WE ARE TRYING TO DETERMINE, SIR.

PREPOSTEROUS!

IS IT?

THEN WHO DO YOU THINK HAD HIS HOTEL ROOM RANSACKED THE NIGHT BEFORE THE BOMBING?

IT WAS?

SOMEONE OBVIOUSLY FELT THERE WAS SOMETHING PRETTY VALUABLE IN THAT ROOM

WHAT DO YOU SUPPOSE THAT MIGHT HAVE BEEN, JOSH?

I'M NOT SURE I LIKE YOUR TONE, COMMANDER!

I GET THAT A LOT!

AND WHO DO YOU THINK PLACED A CELL PHONE CALL THAT SAME NIGHT, FROM YOUR MINISTRY COMPLEX TO A SUSPECTED TERRORIST SAFE HOUSE IN HEBRON?

WHAT?

AS YOU CAN SEE, THERE ARE A LOT OF QUESTIONS THAT STILL NEED ANSWERING.

WOULD YOU CARE TO AMEND YOUR STATEMENT, MINISTER, OR DO WE NEED TO GO TO A HIGHER SECURITY CLEARANCE LEVEL FOR ANSWERS?

NO...NO, OF COURSE NOT!

DEAR GOD, I'LL HELP YOU IN ANY WAY I CAN!

69

CINDY, DID YOU GET THE FEDEX...THE BOOK?

DON'T WORRY TERRY. YOUR BLACK BOOK IS SAFE.

I FOLLOWED YOUR INSTRUCTIONS TO THE LETTER. THE BOOK AND THE RECORDER WERE SHIPPED UP TO MR. MCINTRYE IN NEW YORK.

IF ANYTHING HAPPENS TO EITHER OF US, HE KNOWS WHAT TO DO.

MAC HAS IT?

G, G... GOO' GIRL.

I KNEW I COU' COW ON...COUNT ON YA, YA...YOU.

I THINK THAT'S ENOUGH FOR NOW, MRS. PATEL.

DR. HARPER STILL NEEDS ALL THE REST HE CAN GET.

NURSE WITMAN, YOU READY TO CHANGE HIS I.V.?

YES, DOCTOR.

HOW 'YA DOIN' TERRY?

YEAH, RESS...THAT'S WHAT I NEED RIGHT NOW... RESSS...

BUT WHO ARE ALL THOSE PEOPLE, LUKE?

WHAT PEOPLE?

THAT BIG CROWD OF PEOPLE OVER THERE!

OVER THE NEXT THREE YEARS, AS THE NUMBER OF DISCIPLES IN **THE WAY OF JESUS** CONTINUES TO GROW, THE APOSTLES BEGIN A PROGRAM OF COLLECTING FOOD FROM BELIEVERS AND DISTRIBUTING IT TO THOSE MOST IN NEED....

...LIKE THESE PEOPLE. THE WIDOWS, ORPHANS AND THE POOR

STEP RIGHT UP FOLKS, THERE'S PLENTY FOR ALL!

SO THIS ENORMOUS PROJECT CAN BE HANDLED WITHOUT DIVERTING THE APOSTLES FROM THEIR PRIMARY FOCUS OF PREACHING **THE GOOD NEWS** AND HEALING THE SICK, THEY APPOINT SEVEN MEN TO OVERSEE THIS TASK.

MAY GOD BLESS YOU YOUNG MAN!

ONE OF THE MOST SUCCESSFUL AND ENTHUSIASTIC IN THIS MISSION, IS **STEPHEN**, WHOSE **SPIRITUAL GIFT** IS HIS PASSION FOR HELPING PEOPLE IN NEED.

THOUGH STILL A YOUNG MAN WITH THE FACE THAT WAS SMOOTH LIKE THAT OF AN ANGEL, HE IS **FILLED WITH THE HOLY SPIRIT** AND PERFORMS MANY WONDROUS FEATS AND MIRACULOUS SIGNS AMONG THE PEOPLE.

AS STEPHEN'S INFLUENCE GROWS WITH THE COMMON FOLK, THE PRIESTS OF **THE SYNAGOGUE OF THE FREEMEN** BECOME SO ENVIOUS THAT THEY BRING FALSE TESTIMONY AGAINST HIM, HAVE HIM ARRESTED AND BROUGHT BEFORE THE SANHEDRIN.

THIS BOY IS CONTINUALLY SPEAKING AGAINST THE TEMPLE AND THE LAWS OF MOSES.

WE HAVE EVEN HEARD HIM SAY THAT THIS JESUS **HE WORSHIPS LIKE GOD** WILL DESTROY THE TEMPLE AND CHANGE OUR CUSTOMS.

YOUNG MAN, ARE THESE CHARGES TRUE? SURELY SOMEONE OF YOUR TENDER AGE, WOULD NOT BECOME INVOLVED WITH THE NAZARENE'S ILLEGAL WORSHIP PRACTICES?

STEPHEN RESPONDS TO THESE CHARGES BY AMAZING THESE MEN OF HIGH EDUCATION WITH HIS VAST KNOWLEDGE OF ANCIENT SCRIPTURE...

...AND HISTORY OF THE HEBREW PEOPLE.

AND THEN HE ENRAGES THEM, BY BRINGING CHARGES OF HIS OWN AGAINST THEM.

BROTHERS AND FATHERS, LISTEN TO ME.

YOU ARE A STIFF NECKED PEOPLE, WHO COVER YOUR HEART AND YOUR EARS TO THE TRUTH!

YOU ARE JUST LIKE YOUR FATHERS...ALWAYS RESISTING THE HOLY SPIRIT OF GOD!

WAS THERE EVER A PROPHET YOUR FATHERS DID NOT PERSECUTE? THEY EVEN KILLED THOSE WHO PREDICTED THE COMING OF THE MESSIAH AND NOW YOU HAVE KILLED THE **ANOINTED ONE** HIMSELF!

YOU HAVE RECEIVED THE LAW THAT WAS PUT INTO EFFECT THROUGH ANGELS, BUT HAVE NOT OBEYED IT!

AS JESUS HAS SAID...YOU HAVE LET GO THE COMMANDS OF GOD AND ARE HOLDING ON TO THE TRADITIONS OF MEN!

UPON HEARING THESE CHARGES, ESPECIALLY COMING FROM SUCH A YOUNG MAN, THE COUNCIL BECOMES FURIOUS AND BEGINS TO HURL INSULTS AT STEPHEN.

BUT HE DOES NOT EVEN SEEM TO TAKE NOTICE...

...FOR HE IS FILLED WITH THE HOLY SPIRIT.

LOOK, I SEE HEAVEN OPENING UP TO ME!

JESUS, THE SON OF MAN, IS THERE...

...AND HE IS SEATED AT THE RIGHT HAND OF GOD!

BUT I THOUGHT ONLY PILATE, THE ROMAN GOVERNOR, COULD CONDEMN A MAN TO DEATH IN JERUSALEM?

THAT'S CORRECT, BUT AFTER YEARS OF CONTINUED DEFIANCE BY THIS NOW OUTLAWED SECT, THE CHIEF PRIESTS ARE SO FRUSTRATED THAT ALL THEIR ANGER HAS BEEN FOCUSED ON MAKING AN EXAMPLE OF THIS BOY...DESPITE WHAT ROMAN LAW MAY DICTATE.

STONING HAS BEEN THE ACCEPTED FORM OF CAPITAL PUNISHMENT AMONG THE HEBREWS FOR OVER A THOUSAND YEARS.

AS PRACTICED IN THIS TIME, THE CONDEMNED MAN IS LED TO THE TOP OF A HIGH SCAFFOLD, WHICH IS LOCATED OUTSIDE THE WALLS OF THE CITY.

HE IS THEN STRIPPED AND THROWN OFF THE SCAFFOLD BY THE COUNCIL'S FIRST OFFICIAL WITNESS.

THIS WOULD USUALLY CAUSE AN INJURY GREAT ENOUGH TO PREVENT HIM FROM FLEEING.

THEN, THE COUNCIL'S SECOND OFFICIAL WITNESS DROPS A LARGE CEREMONIAL STONE ONTO THE CONDEMNED MAN'S HEAD FROM ATOP THE SCAFFOLD.

BY THE POWER VESTED IN ME BY GOD AND HIS HOLY COUNCIL, I CONDEMN THIS BOY TO DEATH BY STONING IN ACCORDANCE WITH OUR LAWS.

THEN THE CROWD BEGINS TO HURL HAND-SIZED STONES AT THE CONDEMNED...

...UNTIL HE IS DEAD!

LORD JESUS, RECEIVE MY SPIRIT!

DO NOT HOLD THIS AGAINST THEM, LORD!

IT...

...IS...

...DONE.

AS PART OF THAT PERSECUTION, SAUL AND HIS PHARISEE GUARD GO SYSTEMATICALLY FROM HOUSE TO HOUSE EACH NIGHT IN JERUSALEM, TO ROOT OUT THE SECRET MEETING PLACES OF THE REMAINING FOLLOWERS OF JESUS.

HUNDREDS OF MEN, WOMEN AND CHILDREN ARE IMPRISONED OR KILLED IN THESE RAIDS.

BUT AN UNEXPECTED BENEFIT OF THIS SCATTERING OF DISCIPLES, IS THAT THEY ARE NOW TALKING ABOUT JESUS IN CITIES THAT HAD NOT YET HEARD **THE GOOD NEWS**!

TO COMBAT THIS GROWTH OUTSIDE JUDEA, SAUL PETITIONS THE COUNCIL TO BROADEN HIS AUTHORITY.

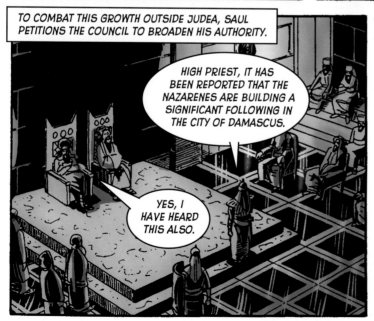

HIGH PRIEST, IT HAS BEEN REPORTED THAT THE NAZARENES ARE BUILDING A SIGNIFICANT FOLLOWING IN THE CITY OF DAMASCUS.

YES, I HAVE HEARD THIS ALSO.

I REQUEST THAT YOU SUPPLY ME WITH LETTERS OF INTRODUCTION, ALONG WITH CONFIRMATION OF MY AUTHORITY FOR THE PRIESTS IN THAT REGION, SO I MAY TAKE PRISONER ANY MAN OR WOMEN WHO IS ACTIVE IN THIS CULT IN THAT AREA.

VERY WELL.

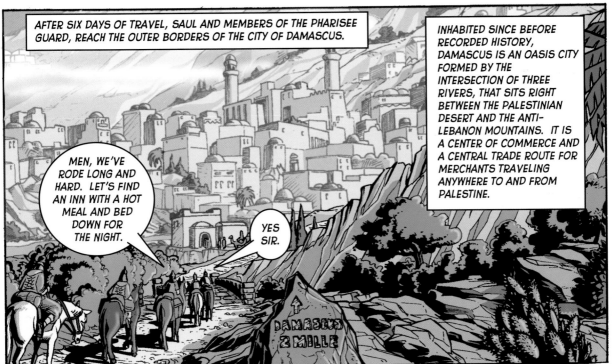

...AFTER YOU MEET A MAN NAMED, ANANIAS.

YE...YE, YES... WHATEVER YOU SAY, MY LORD.

CAPTAIN, WHO ARE YOU TALKING TO?

YOU MEAN YOU D,D...DIDN'T SEE HIM, NOR HEAR HIS WORDS TO ME?

HEAR WHAT? SEE WHO?

IT WAS JE, JE... JESUS OF NAZARETH. HE ACTUALLY SPOKE TO ME FROM THE HEAVENS, GLOWING LIKE AN ANGEL.

BUT SIR, HE'S DEAD AND GONE. YOU'VE TOLD US THAT A HUNDRED TIMES.

YES, YES, I KNOW WHAT I'VE SAID, BUT I,I...I'VE BEEN WRONG...TERRIBLY WRONG!

GAMALIEL WAS RIGHT...I'VE BEEN AT WAR WITH GOD!

CAPTAIN, ARE YOU ALL RIGHT?

NO, I'M NOT. SOMETHING'S DEFINITELY HAPPENED TO ME.

WAS IT THE FALL, SIR?

NO, IT WAS NOT THE FALL.

IT APPEARS THAT I'M NOW T,T... TOTALLY BLIND!

WOW, YOU CAN'T TELL ME SOMETHING LIKE THIS DOES NOT GET HIS ATTENTION!

IT MOST CERTAINLY DOES. IN THE BLINK OF AN EYE, THE SCOURGE OF ALL THINGS RELATED TO JESUS' MINISTRY HAS BECOME A NEW MAN.

HIS LIFE AS SAUL WAS MERELY A PRELUDE TO WHAT IS TO COME, AS GOD'S PLAN FOR HIM BEGINS TO UNFOLD AND REVEALS...

...THE APOSTLE PAUL.

ARE YOU TELLING ME THIS ANTI-JESUS FANATIC BECOMES ONE OF HIS GREATEST ADVOCATES? HOW?

THOSE ANSWERS WILL HAVE TO WAIT, FOR OUR TIME TOGETHER IS JUST ABOUT OVER.

BUT I NEED TO KNOW MORE!

DO NOT WORRY, TERRY...YOU ARE **THE TEMPLE OF THE LIVING GOD**, FOR THE HOLY SPIRIT NOW RESIDES WITHIN YOU.

AND THROUGH THAT SPIRIT, GOD WILL ALWAYS PROVIDE YOU WITH THE ANSWERS YOU SEEK

LUKE, WAIT!

LUKE?

ALL YOU HAVE TO DO IS ASK!

FARE...

BLINK

83

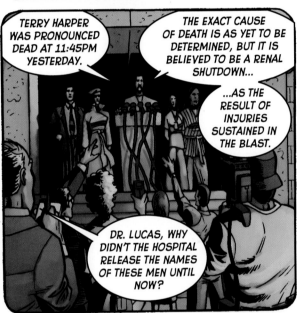

MINUTES LATER...

BEEP
BEEP
BEEP

IT'S ME. HAVE YOU SEEN THE TV THIS MORNING?

NO, NO ONE SUSPECTS A THING.

GOOD. YOU'VE CARRIED OUT YOUR JOB QUITE WELL, RACHEL.

SO NOW YOU'LL GIVE ME MY NATHAN BACK, YES?

YES, WE WILL HONOR OUR PART OF THIS BARGAIN, BUT...

...IF ANYONE FINDS OUT ABOUT OUR LITTLE ARRANGEMENT, YOU'LL NOT ONLY BE ARRESTED FOR MURDER...

...BUT YOUR PRECIOUS NATHAN WILL BE **DEAD!** YOUR SISTER...**DEAD!** YOUR FRIENDS AND CO-WORKERS...**DEAD!**

IS THAT CLEAR, RACHEL?

YES, YES, OF COURSE.

I'M SORRY, I DIDN'T QUITE GET THAT!

A FEW MINUTES LATER....

2 AM, OLD TOWN JERUSALEM.

WATCHMAN ONE, HOW'S IT LOOKING?

CRRKKK... IT'S ALL CLEAR. WE HAVE NO ACTIVITY IN THE PERIMETER... CRRKKK.

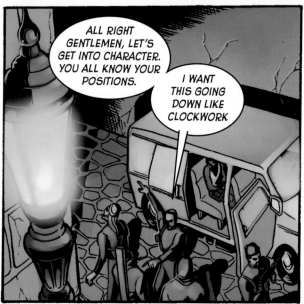

ALL RIGHT GENTLEMEN, LET'S GET INTO CHARACTER. YOU ALL KNOW YOUR POSITIONS.

I WANT THIS GOING DOWN LIKE CLOCKWORK

OKAY...IT'S JUST ABOUT TIME.

COME ON OUT, SPORT.

88

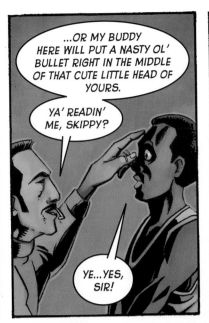

89

CRRKKK...
PEEPING TOM IS
IN POSITION....
CRRKKK!

CRRKKK...
AFFIRMATIVE...
CRRKKK!

YOUR MOM'S
ON HER WAY HERE
RIGHT NOW.

IF YOU KEEP
QUIET, STAY RIGHT IN
THIS SPOT AND DON'T
MOVE, IT'LL ALL BE
OVER IN JUST A
FEW MINUTES.

CAN YOU
DO THAT FOR
ME, TIGER?

YES,
SIR.

GOOD
BOY!

2:32AM

CRRKKK...
PEEPING TOM HAS
ACQUIRED TARGET A.
WAITING ON GREEN LIGHT...
CRRKKK!

CRRKKK...
HAWK ONE ON STATION,
AWAITING ACQUISITION
OF TARGET B...
CRRKKK!

90

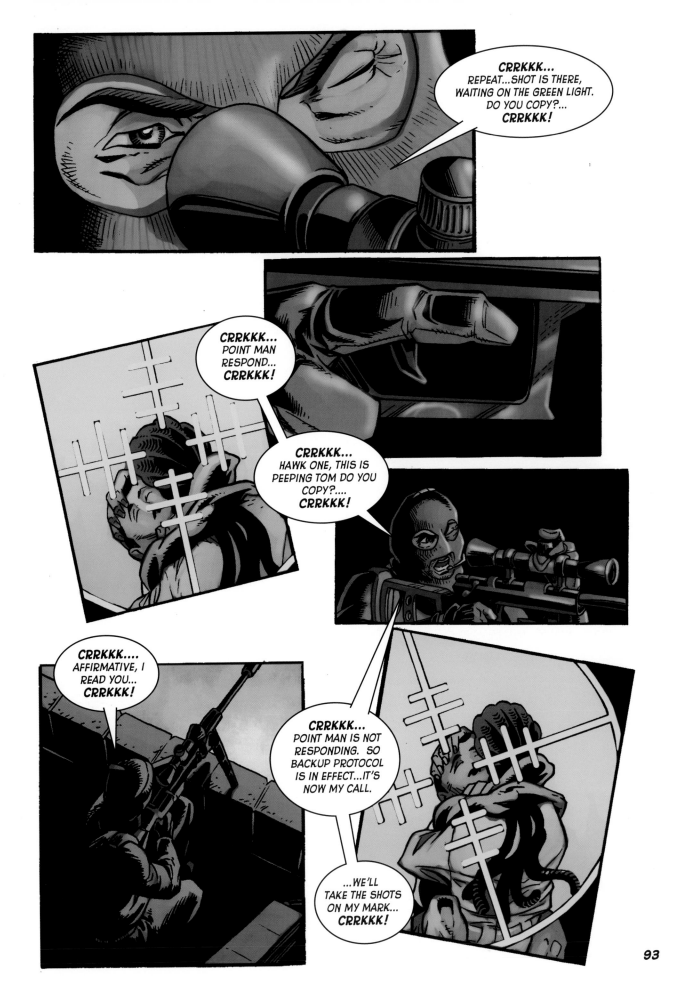

93

THIS APPEARS TO BE ALL OF THEM, COMMANDER ARYEH.

HMMM... I RECOGNIZE THAT ONE FROM INTERPOL FILES.

YOU'RE NOT A TERRORIST...YOU'RE NOT EVEN ARABIAN. YOU'RE NOTHING BUT A MERC!

WHOSE PAYROLL YOU ON THIS WEEK, RICO?

I'VE GOT NOTHING TO SAY TO YOU, COP.

WE'LL SEE ABOUT THAT.

TAKE THEM IN FOR INTERROGATION, BUT KEEP THEM UNDER WRAPS. NO ONE TALKS TO THEM WITHOUT MY SAY SO.

YES, SIR.

RACHEL WITMAN!

WHA...?

IT'S OKAY, WE'RE JERUSALEM POLICE! YOU'RE SAFE NOW.

NO, NO... YOU'VE GOT TO LEAVE!

IF THEY SEE YOU HERE, THEY'LL KILL US...PLEASE GO!

IT'S OKAY, RACHEL...THEY CAN'T HARM YOU ANY MORE. WE'VE GOT 'EM IN CUSTODY.

BUT HOW DID YOU...?

WE WERE TIPPED OFF. THAT'S ABOUT ALL I CAN TELL YOU RIGHT NOW.

THEN YOU KNOW I DIDN'T WANT TO DO IT...THEY MADE ME FEED DR. HARPER THE MERCURY TAINTED I.V.S!

NO NEED TO EXPLAIN RIGHT NOW.

LET'S WORRY ABOUT GETTING YOU AND YOUR SON INTO PROTECTIVE CUSTODY.

95

NEW YORK CITY, THE BOROUGH OF BROOKLYN...12 HOURS EARLIER.

A.N.N. HEADLINES AT THIS HOUR...INTERNATIONAL OUTRAGE CONTINUES TO POUR IN OVER THE DEATHS OF TWO AMERICAN ARCHAEOLOGISTS IN ISRAEL LAST WEEK IN AN APPARENT SUICIDE BOMBING.

SUICIDE BOMBING, MY BUTT!

ISRAELI SECURITY OFFICIALS APPARENTLY HAVE HAD NO LUCK IN DETERMINING WHO'S RESPONSIBLE AND SPECULATION ABOUT THE MOTIVATION BEHIND THE INCIDENT IS RUNNING RAMPANT.

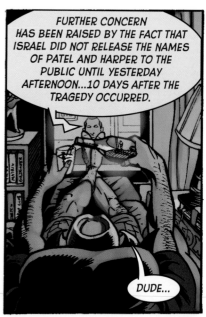

FURTHER CONCERN HAS BEEN RAISED BY THE FACT THAT ISRAEL DID NOT RELEASE THE NAMES OF PATEL AND HARPER TO THE PUBLIC UNTIL YESTERDAY AFTERNOON....10 DAYS AFTER THE TRAGEDY OCCURRED.

DUDE...

IN OTHER INTERNATIONAL NEWS, A WHITE HOUSE SPOKESMAN SAID TODAY THAT...

...WHY'D YOU DO IT?

...THE SURVEILANCE ASPECT OF THE PATRIOT ACT IS JUST A SHORT TERM STRATEGY DESIGNED TO MAINTAIN OUR LEVEL OF SECURITY AGAINST TERRORISTS...

...IT'S NOT AS IF WE'RE GOING TO USE THOSE POWERS TO START SPYING ON AMERICAN CITIZENS OR ANYTHING LIKE THAT!

WHY'D YOU GO IN THERE WITHOUT OL' MAC RIDIN' SHOTGUN?

FRIGGIN' ECHELON!

KNOCK KNOCK

MR. MCINTYRE?

WHATEVER YOU'RE SELLIN', FELLAS, I'M NOT BUYIN'!

WE HAVE A COUPLE OF QUESTIONS AND NEED JUST A MINUTE OF YOUR TIME.

MAY WE COME IN?

96

HADASSAH HOSPITAL, JERUSALEM.

COMMANDER, WHY WAS THE ANTI-TERRORIST UNIT DEPLOYED IN OLD TOWN LAST NIGHT?

WHO IS THAT?

WHY ARE YOU HERE?

NO COMMENT, GENTLEMEN...MAKE A PATH!

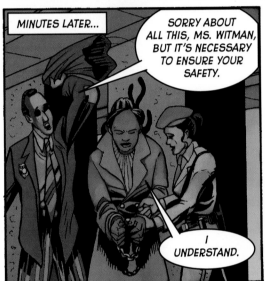

MINUTES LATER...

SORRY ABOUT ALL THIS, MS. WITMAN, BUT IT'S NECESSARY TO ENSURE YOUR SAFETY.

I UNDERSTAND.

BUT WHY'D WE HAVE TO COME HERE?

I FEEL SO ASHAMED. I CAN FEEL THE HATRED IN EVERYONE'S EYES OVER WHAT I'VE DONE!

IT'S IMPORTANT THAT YOU SHOW US EXACTLY WHERE AND HOW THEY WERE TRANSFERRING YOU THE MERCURY TAINTED I.V.S.

BUT I'VE ALREADY TOLD YOU ALL ABOUT THAT IN MY STATEMENT!

YES, I KNOW...

...BUT I'VE FOUND TAKING THE WITNESS BACK AT THE CRIME SCENE HELPS BRING NEW INFORMATION TO LIGHT.

IF YOU SAY SO, COMMANDER...

...ANYTHING I CAN DO TO...?

97

SURPRISE!

END

98

"Whether you turn to the right or to the left, your ears will hear a voice behind you saying, 'This is the way...walk in it!'"

(Book of Isaiah: 30:21)

ADAPTED FROM THE GOSPELS OF:
LUKE, JOHN AND THE BOOK OF ACTS

Glossary of Terms

Annas: High priest of Jerusalem, from A.D. 6-15. Continued to influence policy under his son in law, Caiaphas', priestly leadership.

Blasphemy: Involved direct and explicit abuse of the divine name of God, or claiming divinity.

Caiaphas: High priest of Holy Temple of Jerusalem, from A.D. 18-36. Son-in-law and successor of Annas.

Christ: From the Greek word, translated from the Hebrew, Messiah--meaning "anointed one."

Denarii: A Roman silver coin. One denarius was a day's wage for the ordinary workers and soldiers.

Disciples: One who is taught by another--a learner. He was expected to physically follow his teacher wherever he went, leaving behind both family and occupation.

The Eleven: A reference to Jesus' inner circle of apostles, used after the betrayal/suicide of Judas Iscariot, (#12).

Faith: The complete belief and trust in something, (God), for which there may not exist any objective evidence of proof.

The Freemen: Jewish freed men or descendants of men freed from slavery, who came together in Jerusalem in their own synagogue.

Galilee: The northern region of Palestine that contains Jesus' home village of Nazareth. Area where much of Jesus' public ministry took place.

Gentiles: Any nation or ethnic group outside of the Jews, (Hebrews).

Golgotha: Arabic for, "The place of skulls." The site where crucifixions took place, (including Jesus'), just outside the walls of Jerusalem.

Good News, the: The Gospel or message of Jesus. Specifically the hope and salvation promised to all who believe in his sacrificial death on the cross and resurrection.

James, (the apostle): A Galilean fisherman, brother of the apostle John. Later, leader of the church of Jerusalem.

John, (the apostle): One of Jesus closest disciples and brother of James, he later helped found the church at Jerusalem and later at Ephesus.

Joseph of Arimathea: A respected member of the Jewish ruling council, (the Sanhedrin), he took control of Jesus body after his crucifixion and placed it within his family tomb.

Judas Iscariot: A member of Jesus' inner circle of 12 apostles, who served as their treasurer. He was also a member of the radical sect called Zealots, who desired a violent military style overthrow to the Roman occupation of Palestine.

Koine: A mixture of various languages, (mainly Greek), which became the common man's language in conversation, writing and commerce. It was eventually replaced by Latin.

Mary Magdalene: Became a loyal follower of Jesus after having seven demons cast out her, by him. Stayed with Jesus right up to his physical death on the cross. Was among the first to learn of his resurrection.

Messiah: "The anointed one." The expected deliverer of the Jewish people.

Nazarenes: A derogatory term for followers of Jesus, who was originally from the town of Nazareth.

Nazareth: Jesus' hometown. A small isolated village, located 70 miles north of Jerusalem and 15 miles west of the Sea of Galilee.

Passover: An ancient Jewish festival commemorating the deliverance from Egypt. It was followed immediately by the seven day Feast of Unleavened Bread. The entire festival was often referred to as Passover.

Peter, (Simon): A Galilean fishermen, who was one of Jesus' closest disciples. He became a leader in the early church, and was the first disciple to take the Gospel to the gentiles, (non-Hebrews). His name means, "the rock."

Pharisees: The name means, "the separated ones." The most influential of the Jewish sects, they held strict observance to Mosaic Law and customs and their interpretations of it. The foremost persecutors of Jesus and his followers in Judea.

Pontius Pilate: Roman occupation governor of Judea, from A.D. 26-37.

Rabbi: A title of respect in addressing a Hebrew, (and later), a Jewish teacher of the Torah.

Repentance: A change of mind, purpose and life, (which includes acknowledging one's sin and asking for forgiveness), brought about through connection with God through Christ.

Sacrilege: Desecration of what is held sacred by a culture, religion or movement.

Sadducees: The name means, "righteous ones." A Jewish sect whose membership came mainly from the priesthood and upper classes. They were vigorously opposed to Jesus and his followers..

Son of Man: The name that links Jesus to earth and his mission. It was his favorite designation for himself, (used more than 80 times in the gospels), and emphasizes his humanity and suffering.

Spiritual Gifts: Gifts or talents supernaturally bestowed upon those touched by the Holy Spirit of God, used for sharing the Gospel of Jesus, or to build up his church.

Tarsus: Largest city in the Mediterranean region of Cilicia. It was known as a center of wealth, commerce and its schools of learning, which rivaled those in Athens and Alexandria.

Salvation: In general, a deliverance from evil or danger. A Spiritual rescue from sin and death without redemption.

"Though outwardly we are wasting away, yet inwardly we are being renewed day by day....So fix your eyes not on what is seen, but on what is unseen. For what is seen is temporary, but what is unseen is eternal."

(Book of 2 Corninthians 4:16-18)